W9-CJZ-033

All children have a great ambition to read to themselves...

and a sense of achievement when they can do so. The **read it yourself** series has been devised to satisfy their ambition. Since many children learn from the Ladybird Key Words Reading Scheme, these stories have been based to a large extent on the Key Words List, and the tales chosen are those with which children are likely to be familiar.

The series can of course be used as supplementary reading for any reading scheme. The Elves and the Shoemaker *is intended for children reading up to Book 2c of the Ladybird Reading Scheme. The following words are additional to the vocabulary used at that level –*

shoemaker, wife, his, money, leather, cuts, out, shoes, bed, make, morning, work, sees, did, sells, more, who, us, hide, elves, help, clothes, lot, of, happy

A list of other titles at the same level will be found on the back cover.

The Elves and the Shoemaker

by Fran Hunia
illustrated by John Dyke

Ladybird Books Loughborough

Here is
the shoemaker.

5

This is
the shoemaker's wife.

The shoemaker and his wife have no money.

8

The shoemaker
is in his shop.

He has
some leather.

He cuts out
some shoes.

10

The shoemaker says,
I want
to go to bed.
I can make the shoes
in the morning.

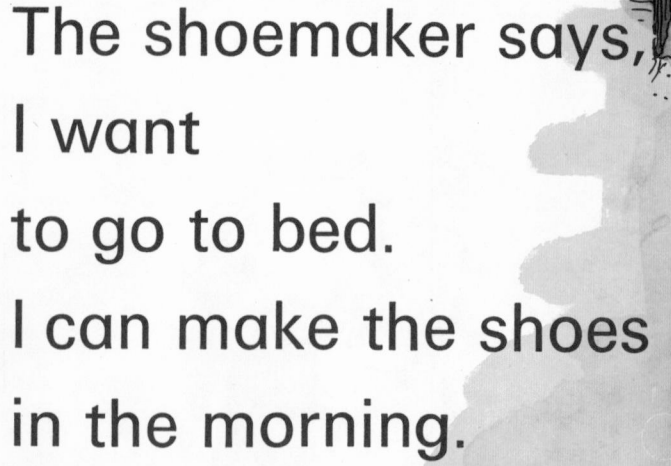

13

In the morning
the shoemaker
comes to work
in his shop.

He sees
some shoes.

He says
to his wife,
Did *you*
make the shoes?

No, says his wife.

The shoemaker
sells the shoes.

He has some money
for more leather.

I can make
some more shoes,
he says.

The shoemaker
cuts out
some more shoes.

He and his wife
go to bed.

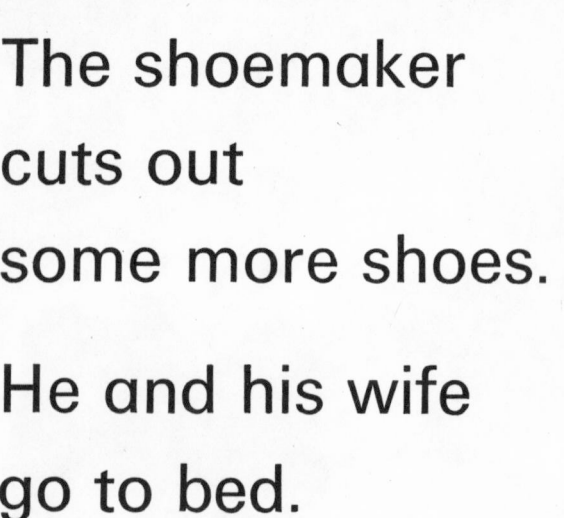

21

In the morning
the shoemaker
comes into his shop
to make the shoes.

22

23

Look,
says the shoemaker.
Did *you*
make the shoes?

No, says his wife.

24

The shoemaker
sells the shoes.

He has some money
for more leather.

26

The shoemaker says,
I want to see
who makes the shoes
for us.
We can hide
and see who comes.

The shoemaker
cuts out
some shoes.

He and his wife hide.

They look to see
who comes.

Some elves come
into the shop.

The elves work
and the shoemaker
and his wife look.

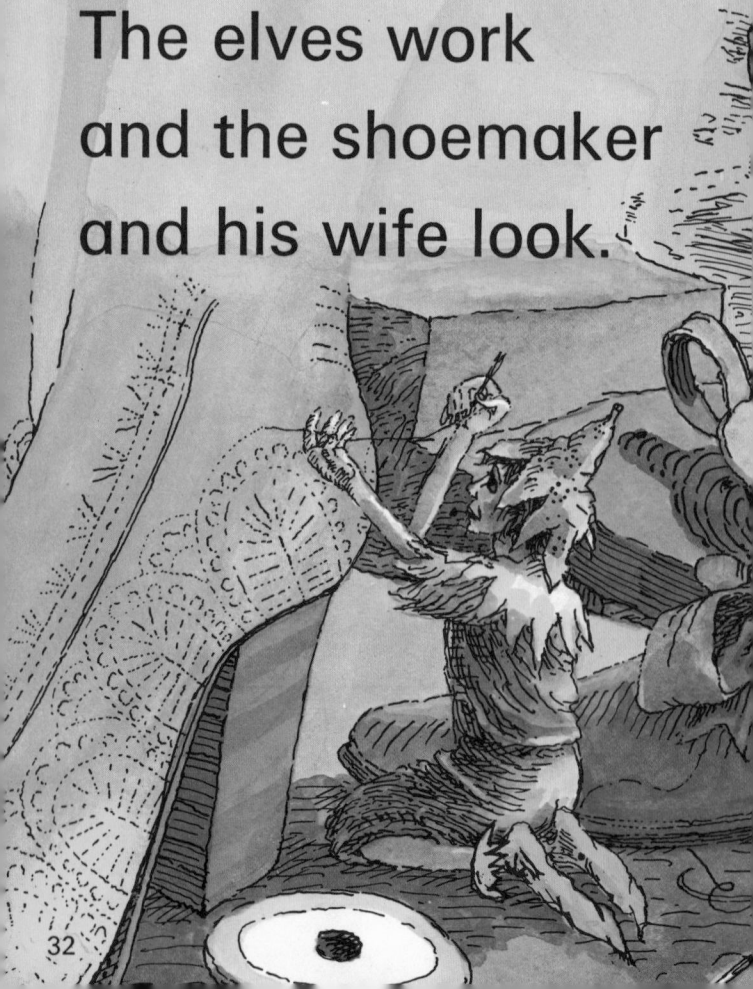

The elves
make the shoes.

The elves
go home.

The shoemaker
and his wife
come out
to see the shoes.

The shoemaker says,
The elves help us.
They make shoes
for us.
I want to help
the elves.

Yes, says his wife.
We can help.
We can make
some clothes
for the elves.

The shoemaker
and his wife
work and work.

They make clothes
and shoes
for the elves.

41

Here are
the clothes
and the shoes.

The shoemaker
and his wife
go and hide.

44

The elves come
into the shop.

Look, they say.
Here are
some clothes
for us.

The elves like
the clothes.

They have fun
in the shop.

48

The elves go home.

They are happy.

The shoemaker
and his wife
have a lot of money
and they are happy.